edward's eyes

edward's eyes

by Patricia MacLachlan

Atheneum Books for Young Readers
New York   London   Toronto   Sydney

Atheneum Books for Young Readers
An imprint of Simon & Schuster Children's Publishing Division
1230 Avenue of the Americas, New York, New York 10020

Book design by Debra Sfetsios
The text for this book is set in Bembo.
Manufactured in the United States of America

10 9 8 7 6 5
Library of Congress Cataloging-in-Publication Data
MacLachlan, Patricia.
Edward's eyes / by Patricia MacLachlan.—1st ed.
p.   cm.
Summary: Edward is one of a large and close family that loves baseball, music, books, and one another, and when he unexpectedly dies and his parents donate his organs, his wonderful eyes got a perfect recipient.
ISBN-13: 978-1-4169-2743-3
ISBN-10: 1-4169-2743-3
[1. Family life—Fiction. 2. Baseball—Fiction. 3. Death—Fiction.
4. Donation of organs, tissues, etc.—Fiction.] I. Title.
PZ7.M2225Ed 2007
[Fic]—dc22   2007010755

For my son John—

who years ago began this story with talk of eyes.
And who lately, all the way from Tanzania, taught me the poetry
of the knuckleball.

With love,
P. M.

edward's eyes

My thanks to:

Elias Reichel, MD,

New England Eye Center, Tufts University School of Medicine, and

Bruce S. Bleiman, MD, Eye Physicians of Northampton.

Thank you to Toni Locke, Jim Locke, and Sandy Warren for their timely poppy story.

Thank you, Albert Groom.

Finally, my heartfelt gratitude to Craig Virden for his years of support, friendship, and eternal good humor.

Prologue

The day was crisp and bright. It was fall on the cape. Maeve had packed us a lunch. She kissed us all, Trick and Albert and me.

"You sure you don't want to come with us?" I asked.

"No, Jake. This is for you," said Maeve with a little smile.

Sabine was in her arms. I kissed her cheek.

The ballpark had painted green walls. The grass was green, too. The seats were not yet filled because we were here early. Trick and Albert Groom and I had come for batting practice.

Some baseball players were out on the field,

throwing baseballs and stretching. Some were doing sprints across the field. We had seats next to the field, by the dugout.

A ball hit the wall in front of us. Albert leaned over and picked it up. He rolled it around in his hands.

"Do you know what is inside a baseball?" he asked me.

I shook my head.

"Charcoal yarn, wrapped up tightly. Yards of it," he said.

He threw the ball back to a baseball player.

It was a good throw. I had never before seen Albert throw a baseball.

"I love the smell of ballparks," said Trick. "Every single one smells the same."

"They do," said Albert.

Some players came close.

Albert Groom touched my arm.

One of the players had protective glasses on.

His hair was brown, cut short. He was tall. When he faced the outfield I could read the name on the back of his shirt.

I stood up.

"Willie?" I called.

He turned and smiled. He waved and turned to go away.

"Do you see the stitches on a knuckleball when it's thrown?" I called.

He stopped. Very slowly he turned and stared at me.

"Can you see the ball leave the pitcher's hand and come down the path to you, like a train coming down the track?"

"Willie?" a player called to him.

Willie waved him away. He walked over to me.

"Yes," he said softly.

"Do you hit better now than you ever did before?"

"Yes."

It was a whisper.

"My brother Edward learned how to throw a knuckleball. And he never ever once struck out," I said.

"Edward," he said. "So that's his name."

Chapter 1

My earliest memory begins with Edward, *as if somehow I have no life to remember before him. The memory comes to me often, mostly at night, but more often during the day now, surprising me. It is a very early memory. Not as early as the artist, Salvador Dali, my sister Sola tells me. He could remember when he was inside his mother, Sola says, where the world looked flat, like squashed egg.*

But this is my memory:

Maeve and Jack have just brought baby Edward home from the hospital. Maeve and Jack are our parents, but we don't call them Mom and Dad, except for Edward, who when he learns to talk will speak to them in a formal manner, a bit English. "Motha and Fatha," he will say in his little tin voice.

Here's the scene:

Maeve and Jack walk in the front door, Maeve carrying baby Edward in his green blanket, packed tightly like a pickle in plastic. I am only three years old, but I can tell from their faces that Maeve and Jack want us to love Edward. They look a little happy, but not too happy; a little fearful as if they are adding an unwanted puppy to our large litter. Sola, the oldest, is used to this. Edward is the fourth baby they've brought home to her. Will, seven, is interested for only the barest moment, then he goes off to read a book in the corner, to spend the day happily in his own head. Wren, not yet five, reaches out to brush Edward's face with her hand. Maeve and Jack like this, a physical sign of affection. They look at me then.

"Jake?" says Maeve.

They wait. I peer down at Edward, my face close to his.

"He will poop all day long. And throw up," Will says.

Wren bursts into laughter at the sound of the word "poop." Sola, having heard years of this talk, unscrews the top of her fingernail polish calmly. Will goes back to his book. He turns a page.

"Jake?" repeats Maeve.

And when I don't say anything she hands me Edward. Just like that. As if he were a bundle or a book. I remember sitting very still, so scared I can't move. And then it happens. Edward opens his eyes and looks at me. His eyes are the dark mud-blue of the night sky, but there are surprising little flecks of gold in them. They stare right into my eyes. My heart begins to beat faster. I try to say something. I want to say that Edward is beautiful . . . the most beautiful thing I have ever seen. I want to say that I love him more than anything or anyone I know. But I am only three, and when I try to talk I can't say all those words.

"His eyes," I begin.

Maeve reaches out and smooths my hair. Her hand is cool and she smiles at me because she already knows what I can't say. Tears sting at the corners of my *eyes. Maeve takes us both—Edward and me—into her arms.*

"Edward's eyes," I say into her shoulder, the tears coming at last. "Edward's eyes."

Edward is little.

I sat on the floor, leaning against the bathtub, trying to do my homework. Maeve sent me to check on Edward.

"Do it, Edward."

He sat on the toilet, his legs dangling.

"Where's Motha?" he asked.

"In the kitchen."

"Read to me," said Edward.

"Please."

"Please," repeated Edward.

I picked up one of his books. I didn't need to look at it. I knew it by heart. I closed my eyes. "In the great green room there was a telephone . . ."

"French, maybe," said Edward. Edward loved French.

I smiled. Edward was so used to hearing all of us talk that he often used words like "maybe" and "actually" and "perhaps."

"Dans la grande chambre verte il y a un téléphone . . ."

"What's that?" asked Edward, pointing to another book.

I picked up the baseball rule book.

"'The infield fly rule in baseball,'" I read. "'The infield fly rule is there to prevent advantage to the fielders in a baseball game. The rule goes into effect when there are fewer than two outs and there are players on first and second base, *or* on first, second and third base. If it is a fair fly ball in the infield, the umpire can call "infield fly" or "batter is out!" whether or not the ball is caught.'"

"Now do it," I said.

"Why?"

"Because everyone does it."

"Maybe I don't want to," said Edward.

I sighed.

"If you don't go I'll leave you here to get a ring around your bottom."

"Actually, I have one," he said.

Sola appeared in the doorway.

"Where's Maeve? Where's Jack? What am I doing sitting here?" I said to her.

"Your turn," said Sola. "I did it. Will and Wren did it. This family is a democracy."

"Edward, please!" I pleaded.

"I want a dollar," said Edward.

Sola bursts into laughter. She pulls a bill out of her jean pocket and hands it to him. We can hear her laughing down the hallway. Then it is silent in the bathroom. Edward looks at me for a moment, those blue eyes staring into mine. Then he jumps down from the toilet and flushes it.

He hands me the dollar.

"I went a long time ago," he says. "This is yours."

Edward walks out the door and down the hallway. Then I hear him walking back. He stands in the doorway.

"The infield fly rule is not dumb, you know," he announces.

It is Edward's first day of kindergarten.

"We'll walk you to school, Edward," said Wren.

"I know the way," said Edward. "I'll walk ahead of you. Two steps."

Edward held up two fingers.

Maeve looked a little sad.

"Oh, I thought I'd walk with you, Edward," she said.

Edward shook his head, making Jack smile.

"You're busy," he said to Maeve, not unkindly.

Edward picked up his navy blue backpack with RED SOX on it. He wore a blue and white striped shirt and jeans. His light brown hair was smooth.

He smiled at all of us.

"Let's go," he said cheerfully.

Maeve bit her lip as if she might cry. Edward looked at her.

"You can walk with me tomorrow," he whispered.

Maeve burst into tears. Jack got up and swung Maeve around in the kitchen until she laughed.

"Out, out, all of you," he said. "Maeve will be fine. We'll put on music and dance in the kitchen. Maybe we'll eat ice cream!"

Jack shooed us out the door and we marched down the steps and across the yard. Behind us, in the kitchen, music started.

Edward turned around, two steps ahead of us, and walked backward.

"Tina Turner," he announced. He sang, "What's love got to do with it?"

"Some day I'll write a book about this," said Will.

We were all surprised. Will didn't talk very much. His look was very serious as he watched Edward.

"I bet you will," said Sola, putting an arm around him.

"Edward's not nervous or scared," says Wren very

softly. "I was scared my first day of school. I'm a little scared today."

She pauses, then looks at me.

"Edward's not scared of anything," she said.

"No. He's not," I say to her. "He's not."

Edward leads us the five blocks to school.

What's love got to do with it?

When Edward is in third grade he begins to stay up later at night than I do. On my way to bed I hear whispering on the porch. A moon shines over the water.

"So when I die," says Wren, "I'm coming back as a bird. Or maybe a dog. Nobody's happier than Weezer."

It is quiet.

"What about you?" she whispers.

"A fish," says Edward promptly. "I'll be in the ocean. I'll come in and go out with the tides."

Wren is silent. I keep listening. But talk is over.

Then, just as I walk away, I hear Edward say, "In and out, in and out, in and out," three times.

Chapter 2

It was dusk and the water was flat and shining. Albert Groom and I were watching the daily summer baseball game in the front yard. Albert's dog, Weezer, lurked in the outfield.

"Weezer thinks he's an outfielder," said Albert softly.

"He is," I said. "He gets to the ball faster than Wayne."

"That's because Wayne is too busy picking his nose," commented Albert.

"Don't you want to play?" Albert asked me.

"I like to watch," I said. "And these are all Edward's friends."

"Too young for you?" asked Albert, smiling.

"No. I just like to watch," I said. "Like you."

"Well, I would play right now if my legs would make it around the bases," said Albert.

"I watch," I said.

"We'll watch then," said Albert.

Albert's voice was musical, as if he might begin singing. His dark skin was almost blue black in the late light. Edward called Albert African-American. Albert called himself black. He had played baseball years ago. And his father, Trick, before him, had played in the Negro League. Every time there was a game in our front yard Albert was there on our porch, watching intently, as if it were a championship. His hand rested on his wooden cane.

Edward's friends were playing: Wayne, Billy Bob, Mavis, who was the best catcher, Lulu and Mary Brigid and Lukie and Morris and Ted and Brendan and Caitlin and Joe.

Edward walked to the plate. One out. Lukie

and Mary Brigid on base. Edward was the best hitter.

"Edward says he can see the ball coming," I said. "He can see the path it's going to take, like a train on a track."

It was true. Edward, in his entire eight years, had never once struck out.

"Those eyes," said Albert admiringly, his voice so soft. "Those wonderful eyes," he repeated in a whisper.

There was a crack sound of ball on wood. Edward hit a pop-up.

"Infield fly rule!" he cried happily, looking at me as if he had invented it himself.

Mavis dropped her blankie and came up to bat.

"Batter, batter, batter," yelled Mary Brigid.

The sun went down. Weezer howled in the outfield, wishing for a long hit.

Mavis grounded out. She picked up her blankie. Everyone went home for dinner.

"See you tomorrow," said Albert. He walked down the steps and went out to get Weezer, who would wait all night under the moon if Albert didn't take him home.

"Bonsoir, Albert Groom," called Edward. "Bonsoir!"

The game was over.

Chapter 3

"Did you live by the sea when you were little?"

I woke up, hearing Edward's voice through my open window. When I looked out I could see Edward and Albert sitting on the porch.

"I was born by the sea," said Albert.

"How old are you?" asked Edward.

Edward always asked Albert personal questions. He asked him anything and all things. He loved Albert. And Albert always told Edward the truth.

"Sixty-eight," said Albert.

"Is that old?" asked Edward.

"Not to my father," said Albert.

Albert's father, Trick, was ninety years old. He spent time walking around town, carrying a bag of pretzels and taking notes about everything he saw.

In the distance I saw Sola and Wren swimming, only their heads showing. They looked like sea otters. Albert's dog, Weezer, was swimming, too. Weezer came out of the water and started up the grass lawn to the house.

"Run!" called Albert.

Albert and Edward pushed back their chairs, and I heard the slam of the screen door.

Downstairs, Albert and Edward stood at the door, looking out. Maeve was playing music in the kitchen. James Taylor sang while she danced. I knew she was dancing even though I couldn't see her. Maeve always danced.

"I've seen fire and I've seen rain. . . ."

"But I always thought that I'd see you again," Albert sang with James Taylor. He smiled when he saw me on the stairs.

"Morning, Jake."

"Morning."

Light came through the screen, making crisscrosses on Albert's face.

"Is it safe to go out now?" whispered Edward.

Albert shrugged.

"We'll see," he said, pushing open the screen door.

I could still hear Maeve, in the kitchen, singing along with James Taylor.

Weezer, closer than they think, shakes seawater all over Albert and Edward.

"Weezer! Dumb old boy!" shouts Albert.

Edward's laughter mixes with my mother's music. Always, always, when Maeve sings I hear Edward's laughter. For the rest of my life.

Always.

"But I always thought that I'd see you again."

Chapter 4

"Summer!" called Jack. He came up the hill with a box.

Sola and Wren hurried out of the water. Will left his window seat in the living room to come out to the porch.

"Books," Will whispered. He grinned.

Summer always smelled like heat, the ocean, and the spines of old books.

Jack set the large box of books on the porch.

"My favorite!" I said, picking up a copy of *Treasure Island*.

"You read that last year," said Will, digging through the box.

"I'll read it again," I said. "I'll read it next year, too."

"I know," said Will, smiling.

Albert Groom sat on the steps, waiting for the next baseball game to begin.

"How to Pitch," said Edward happily, holding up a book.

He handed the book to Albert.

"Ah," said Albert. He opened the book.

"The knuckleball," he said softly, so softly that everyone looked at him. "One of life's mysteries. Think of it, the pitcher flips it toward home plate; it has no spin and you can't hit it. I've always thought of the knuckleball as a kind of Zen experience," he said.

Jack smiled and sat back.

"We live on a sphere which is spinning 1,000 miles per hour, in a galaxy which is spinning," said Albert. "Our bodies are made of molecules whose electrons are all spinning and orbiting. And with all this, and a small flip of the fingers and wrist, a round ball is thrown with zero spin."

He looked up suddenly.

"A mystery."

"A mystery," repeated Edward, staring at Albert.

Every summer Jack and Maeve took time off from the bookstore, hiring college students who read the summer away, room by room, from history to architecture to bee-keeping.

"They fall in love," said Jack, "with Chekhov and Shakespeare and Margaret Wise Brown."

"And with each other," said Maeve, music following her as she came out of the house. "In the heat. Jack doesn't believe in air-conditioning," she told Albert.

"It's unromantic," said Jack, making Albert smile.

"Oh?" Maeve commented, her eyebrows raised. "Sweat is romantic?"

Jack and Maeve looked at each other and we'd roll our eyes and smirk, somehow knowing that they had fallen in love between the rows of books, too. Probably sweating, the two of them.

"Have you ever been in love?" Edward asked Albert.

"Edward, that's private," said Maeve.

Albert smiled. "That's all right, Maeve."

"Many times," he said to Edward. "Sometimes, on the baseball field, I'd look over into the stands and a girl would be looking back at me. Sometimes, it was as if we were the only ones there, no one else around. Until a fly ball came, of course," he added.

"That is very romantic, Albert," said Maeve.

"So you never got married?" I asked.

"I was married to baseball," said Albert.

"Me, too," said Edward.

Everyone laughed.

Will found two more books at the bottom of the box.

"This is better than Christmas," he said.

I picked up a book on the animals of Africa.

"Better than birthdays," I said. "Better than most anything."

And it was, rummaging around boxes of books, squirreling away books in our rooms, treasures waiting to be discovered and traded, read and reread.

In the summer Maeve tossed a flowered table-cloth over the television set, serving teas in the afternoons with little cucumber and watercress sandwiches with the crusts cut off, bowls of chocolates and jelly beans, mostly red, and cookies. There were black and green olives, and salads with strange names like endive and radicchio with raspberry and walnut dressing, and for all of us, cakes that were Maeve's trademark. She was not a good cook, Maeve, but she made tea cakes with chocolate and marshmallow and almond cream icing topped with candied decorations. I don't think they were baked. Wren once said that they had to harden out of boredom, standing around in the summer heat. They were sweet, though, so sweet that we had to eat them with glasses of ice water lined up in a row to wash away the sugar. Even Sola, the true sweet eater of the family, couldn't eat more than one. After one "coma cake," as Sola called it, she would stagger to the porch hammock strung between two white pillars.

"Don't touch me," she'd warn us, her arms over her eyes. "Don't even speak to me. And do not swing the hammock. I'll be sick."

The rest of us, by that time, were so energized by sugar that we went outside to run around violently in the heat, sometimes playing soccer. Before the sun went down Maeve would come out to hit us baseballs with the fungo bat. We chased baseballs until by dusk we lay in exhausted heaps.

Out over the water there was an orange full moon above, a watery one below. Edward put his head on my shoulder, and the air was still. Then, one by one by one, the lightning bugs came out.

"Are you asleep, Edward?" I whispered.

"Yes, I am," said Edward, making me laugh.

Sometimes Maeve and Jack would lead us off to bed. But most times, if there wasn't rain coming, they would toss blankets over us and we'd sleep outside, Edward's head on my shoulder, his sweet-smelling breath soft on my neck.

Chapter 5

"What are you doing?" I asked.

Wren, Will and Edward were behind the barn, Wren hunkered down behind a home plate bag, Will sitting to the side reading aloud, Edward pitching.

Will looked at me for a moment as he read.

"The ball should be held as shown ... clenching the ball with your bent fingers. . . ."

He got up and went over, showing a picture to Edward.

Edward nodded.

"I'm learning to throw a new pitch," said Edward. "I'm going to surprise Albert Groom on his birthday."

I smiled. Edward often used Albert's whole name. It was as if Edward liked to say it. Albert Groom.

"What pitch?" I asked. Edward tried all things. Even a new pitch.

"You'll see," said Edward. "Ready?" he called to Wren.

Wren grinned.

"It's only a Wiffle ball, Edward. You're not going to hurt me."

Edward threw a slow-looking, loopy pitch.

Wren caught it and stood.

"That's very odd, Edward," she said.

"What do you mean?"

"No spin," she said. "No spin at all. And it dipped."

Edward smiled.

"It says here in this book," said Will, "that Annabelle Lefty Lee once threw a perfect game when she played in the women's league. She threw a knuckleball. It says here that if it works batters can't hit it. If it doesn't even the pitcher doesn't know where it's going."

"Risky," said Edward. "I like that."

"Not afraid of anything," Wren said to me.

"It doesn't *look* very hard to hit," I said. "It looks slow and easy."

Edward looked at me.

"Come on, Jake." He beckoned. "You try."

I shook my head.

"I'm not a good hitter," I said.

"Doesn't matter," said Edward with a grin. "You won't hit this anyway. No one can. Come on," he repeated.

I picked up the bat and stood in the batter's box.

"You're going to love this," said Edward.

He threw the ball. It seemed to come slowly, and I cocked the bat and swung. And missed.

Will laughed.

"Doesn't look too hard to hit," he said.

"Don't mock me," I said. "Throw it again, Edward."

He threw.

"Strike two," he said as I swung and missed.

"Strike three."

"Strike four."

"Strike five."

Wren and Will fell over laughing at me.

"Albert Groom is going to be very surprised," said Edward.

It rained for a week, so there were no baseball games. But that didn't stop Edward. He practiced his new pitch every day, no umbrella. He begged Will, Wren and me to practice with him. And we did. Sola refused. He threw Wiffle balls at first, and then he went to a tennis ball. Finally, in the drizzle of late June, Wren's hair all curly from the humidity, we stood behind the barn, and Edward threw his first baseball knuckleball to Wren.

* * *

I stand behind the plate and watch. It is almost as if it happens in slow motion, this ball coming so slowly that we seem to wait forever for it. I can even see the stitching on the ball. And then it darts past Wren. Past me.

Will didn't say anything. Wren didn't say anything. I just looked at Edward and smiled. He smiled back.

"Right behind you, Annabelle Lefty Lee," he said.

Finally the rain ended. Jack and Maeve joined Albert Groom and me on the porch to watch the game. The sky was overcast, clouds moving in over the water.

"Rain again, maybe," said Jack.

"I hope not," I said. "Edward has a surprise."

Albert's hand rested on Weezer.

"What kind of surprise?" Albert asked.

"The best," I said.

Albert turned to look at me.

"The best?" said Albert, smiling. "What can that be, Weezer?" Weezer thumped his tail against the porch floor. Mavis came with her blankie. Mary Brigid came wearing a dress.

"I have to go to a party after the game," she complained.

"Very nice," said Maeve.

"Sort of lends a formal quality," said Albert Groom. Wayne, Billy Bob, Lukie, and Morris, Brendan and Caitlin came.

Weezer whined.

"All right," said Albert. "Go out there."

Weezer loped out to center field, turned and sat. Mavis and Joe laughed. The sun broke through, and Trick came up the side lawn.

"Have a seat, Trick," said Jack.

"I will," said Trick. "Weezer playing?"

"Very funny," said Albert.

Trick winked at me.

"Play ball," yelled Trick.

Edward smiled at him, then at Albert, and at me. He walked to the pitcher's mound.

I heard Albert take a breath. "Edward's *pitching*? He's not a pitcher."

Wren came to sit on the steps, Will next to her. Even Sola came out on the porch and leaned against the wall.

The game began in sunlight.

Edward threw his first pitch.

"Hey!" called Mary Brigid. "What *was* that?"

Albert sat up straight and peered at Edward.

"Hey," called Trick, imitating Mary Brigid, "that was a knuckleball!"

"When did this happen?" whispered Albert.

"All through the week of rain," I told him. "He practiced every day."

"A knuckleball is almost impossible to catch," said Wren. "But I got pretty good at it. Even in the rain."

Albert smiled at her.

"Good for you."

Edward threw two more knuckleballs. Three strikes. Mary Brigid was out.

Wayne, Billy Bob and Mavis were out, too. And Mary Brigid again.

Finally Wayne, frustrated, threw his bat at the ball, surprisingly hitting it into the outfield. Weezer grabbed the ball and ran down to the water, prancing along the edges of the water.

Edward walked over to the porch.

"I learned to do it," he told Albert, "but it's still a mystery."

"Yes," said Albert, beaming.

"Happy birthday, Albert Groom," Edward said.

Chapter 6

It happened on the Fourth of July. How was it we didn't notice? All the signs were there. At least Sola said so later, and she had been through this many times. But we were surprised. Even Sola.

It was cool for July. As the sun went down we all sat out on the front lawn, our bellies full of hamburgers, hot dogs and cake. Albert Groom and Trick, Maeve and Jack sat in chairs; the rest of us wrapped in blankets. Above, the fireworks bloomed over the water; sparkling dandelions in the sky and in the water below.

"I wish we could have fireworks every day," said Edward, curled up between Sola and me.

"That would be superfluous," said Sola. She turned to Edward. "One of the few vocabulary words I remember."

Edward smiled. I could see his white teeth in the dark.

"Fireworks are never superfluous," he said. "We should have them at every event."

He began to list firework events.

"Deaths, birthdays, end of school, beginning of school, first case of poison ivy, first knuckleball thrown . . ."

"Beginning a book," continued Will.

"Finishing a book," said Jack, laughing.

"Reading a book again," I said.

"New boyfriend," said Sola, making us laugh.

"A perfect baseball game," said Trick.

"*Any* baseball game," said Albert.

There was a sudden silence between fireworks.

"Birth, you forgot," said Maeve, her voice suddenly strange and soft in the silence, a faraway sound to it.

We turned our heads to look at her. Even Albert stared. Then, he reached out and took Maeve's hand. He smiled at her.

"What?" said Will.

"Isn't that nice," said Albert.

"What? What is nice?" demanded Wren.

Sola sighed. She pulled the blanket over her head.

"A new baby," she said under the blanket. "Yet . . . Another . . . Baby." She spaced out the words as if she were making a pronouncement.

"No," I said. "No."

"It's true," said Maeve. "Remember how you loved Edward the moment he came home, Jake?"

"That's different," I said loudly. "That was Edward!"

"Wait!" said Edward, sitting up. "Can we have fireworks when she is born?"

"She?" said Sola.

"Yes," said Edward with a great smile. "It will be a girl. Can we name her Sabine?"

"French," said Trick.

"She'll be Sabine. And we'll have fireworks!" said Edward.

Now it was everyone's turn to stare at Edward. There was, in his voice, the feel of sunlight, even though it was dark.

And then, a great shooting fireworks went up and filled the sky, sparks falling down to the water like bright rain.

"Fireworks, remember," Edward said to Maeve.

Chapter 7

"What is Trick doing?" asked Edward.

Edward, Albert and I were in the rowboat, handheld fishing lines dropped over the sides. The water was still. The sky was summer blue, with two high white clouds. Edward pointed to the shore with his chin. Trick sat on a rock, staring out over the water.

"Looking for signs," said Albert. "Trick looks for signs all the time. Most times he finds them."

"What do you mean, signs?" I asked.

"Things happen to point you in one direction or another," said Albert. "You just have to look for them."

"Signs," said Edward, thoughtfully.

"Well, there were no signs Maeve was going to have a baby," I said.

"Sabine," corrected Edward.

Albert smiled.

"Whatever," I said. "At least we weren't paying attention to signs."

"Well, Trick does," said Albert.

Edward bobbed his fishing line up and down. He looked at Trick.

Suddenly, Edward handed me his fishing line and stood up, rocking the rowboat a little.

"Edward!" I said, holding on to the gunwales of the boat.

Edward stripped off his shirt and pants until he stood in his shorts. His eyes were the color of the sky.

"What are you doing?"

"I'm giving Trick a sign!"

And Edward dove a perfect dive, slipping quietly into the water, rocking the boat a little as he went. Trick watched as Edward swam across the inlet. His strokes were smooth and steady, and Trick watched him as he came to the shore.

"He can do anything, Edward," I said softly.

Beside me Albert bobbed his fishing line up and down.

"Seems so," he said. "That's because Edward tries to do everything. He doesn't care if it doesn't work."

"You mean fail?" I asked.

Albert smiled.

"I don't think Edward thinks of it as failure. He thinks of it as not working when it doesn't. What he does doesn't define him."

"Well, what does?" I asked.

"The trying of it," said Albert.

"Who is he?" I said very softly.

It wasn't a question, and Albert didn't take it as one. He kept bobbing his fishing line up and down. A small cloud tried to cover the sun, and there was a moment of quiet coolness. A sign?

"He's going somewhere," said Albert. "Somewhere he knows, or maybe doesn't. But he's going somewhere."

The cloud passed. The sun came out. And Edward sat down on a rock next to Trick.

It is like watching slow motion; like looking at one of Edward's knuckleballs coming to the plate. Edward leans over and says something, the sun making his hair as light as water. Trick, listening, suddenly throws back his head and laughs. Albert and I can hear his laughter come across the water, as clear as if he were next to us.

Signs?

Clouds over the sun?

Birds flying in the outfield?

Trick's signs.

Edward's signs.

Where is my sign?

✳ ✳ ✳

We rode our bikes to town, Edward riding circles around me as he always did, speeding ahead, then falling back. He waved at neighbors.

"Watch where you're going, Edward," I said.

"I know where I'm going," he said with a smile.

"You have the list?"

Edward reached in his pocket and held the list up in his hand. It fell from his hand and the wind whipped it past me.

"Edward!"

"I'll get it," he said, and fell back again, riding back to where the list lay in the road.

"Look! I'm a circus rider!" he called, leaning down to pick it up as he rode.

"You belong in a circus all right," I told him.

When Edward put his brakes on, coming into town, they made a sudden grinding sound. I reached out and grabbed his belt to slow him down.

"I've got you," I said. "You'd better fix those brakes."

When we had bought the things on the list we rode home side by side. At the hill leading down to our house, I reached out and held his belt again.

"I'll save you," I said.

"Merci," said Edward.

Chapter 8

Game time.

Jack was grilling chicken to celebrate fall. The smell of it drifted across the yard along with Maeve's music.

"I hear Emmylou Harris in the kitchen," said Albert.

"Yes," said Jack at the grill. "She's been there all morning with Maeve."

"On the wings of a snow-white dove," sang Albert very softly.

It was the sixth inning of the front yard game. It would go seven innings unless the chicken was done first.

"Is this game tied or what?" I asked.

"Hard to know," said Albert. "There's a bit of creative scoring going on here."

"Maybe that's because no one really cares who wins," I said. "Edward doesn't care, anyway."

"True," said Albert. "For Edward it's the game that counts. Not the score."

"It's six to six," said Trick. "I've got it written down."

He held up his notebook.

Edward came up to bat.

Mary Brigid was pitching. She wound up and threw one past Edward.

Edward grinned.

"Nice pitch!" called Albert, surprised.

"Edward taught me," Mary Brigid called back.

Albert smiled.

"I'll say he did," he said.

"Here comes strike three," yelled Mary Brigid.

"I don't think so," said Edward.

A gull flew low over the outfield.

"See that gull?" called Edward. "That's a sign."

Mary Brigid threw. Edward hit a line drive past Mary Brigid, past Caitlin at second base, and between Wayne and a surprised Weezer in the outfield. Just where the gull had been.

"Some sign," said Trick.

"He placed that one," said Albert. "Those wonderful eyes."

Edward stood on second base and waved at us on the porch.

Maeve came out on the porch and waved back.

"Nice hit," she called to Edward.

"Chicken's ready," called Jack.

"Wait!" shouted Edward. "Hit me home, Mavis!"

Mavis stepped up to the plate. She wagged the bat at Mary Brigid. "C'mon, pitcher girl!"

Mary Brigid pitched, and Mavis hit a hard drive past Billy Bob and the shortstop and out into the grass. Edward ran to third, looked back once, and rounded third and slid home, feet first, on the grass.

He stood up, grass stains on his pants, grass and dirt in his hair.

"Did you see that, Trick? That sign?" called Edward.

"Give me five," said Trick.

Edward came over, sweat glistening on his face, and slapped hands with Trick.

"You won the game," said Trick.

"Oh?" said Edward. "Well, that's all right . . . but," and he looked up at us, his blue eyes bright in the sunlight, "it was a great game!"

Albert didn't turn to look at me, but I heard his whisper.

"See? It's always the game."

Chicken, roasted corn, salad, and chocolate cake. It was dusk and Maeve and Jack picked up plates, Sola, Wren and Will helping. Maeve seemed big to me all of a sudden.

"I hardly noticed before that she was going to have a baby," I said.

Albert looked at Maeve.

"It's like old age. You don't see it coming. Then one day you look in the mirror and see your father."

"No you don't," said Trick. "I do."

We laughed.

"She'll have Sabine soon," said Edward.

"You are so sure? That it's Sabine?" I asked.

Edward nodded, a small smear of chocolate at the corner of his mouth. "I've seen signs."

"What signs?" I asked.

"You'll know them when you see them, Jake," said Edward.

"What signs?" I asked Trick.

"It's like Edward says. You see them. You know them," said Trick.

He leaned back against the porch railing. The moon was big and orange over the water behind him.

Signs.

Pooh.

Chapter 9

It was night, no moon that I could see. The four of us were in Sola's room taking bets on when Maeve would have the baby.

"I pick the last week of November," said Wren. "She'll have it early, right in the middle of Thanksgiving."

"Cynic," said Sola, smiling.

"December 5," said Will. "She'll be late and cranky."

"But she'll still sing," said Edward, cheerfully.

"Have you noticed," I said, "that she brings our babies home and lets us raise them? That's what she did with you," I said to Edward. "She popped you onto my lap."

"You said 'our' babies," said Edward. "Sabine will be mine. I'll get to read the rules of baseball to her. Like you did. And read her *Goodnight Moon* in French. She'll already know French, of course," he said quickly.

Wren burst out laughing.

"Born knowing French? That's ridiculous," she said.

"Mais non," said Edward.

He grinned.

"And I will teach her how to ride a bike," he said.

"And read a book," said Will.

"And go to the bathroom," I said.

"*And.*" Edward stood up. "And to throw a knuckleball!"

I tackled Edward, and we rolled around on the bed, Edward laughing.

"So, when do *you* think the baby will be born?" I asked Edward.

Edward sat up.

"Sooner than you think," he said.

"What do you mean, sooner?" I asked.

"Soon."

"How do you know that?"

"Signs," we all said together.

"Jake."

A hand touched my shoulder. I turned over, confused.

There was a piece of moon over the water.

"What? What's wrong?"

"Sabine's coming," Edward whispered.

"What!" I sat up. "How do you know?"

"Mother's packing her suitcase," he whispered.

"It's still November. Isn't it early?" I asked. "What does Sola say?"

"Sola told me to go back to bed," said Edward.

I couldn't help smiling. That sounded like Sola. Outside, Jack's car started up. Edward and I scrambled over the bed to the window and watched it slowly move away.

"I'm going," said Edward.

"You can't do that! You can't ride your bike in the middle of the night."

"I'll walk," said Edward. "I have to be there. For Sabine."

"It's three miles," I said. "And it's cold."

"I'm going," said Edward.

He ran out of the room. I stood up and pushed back the covers.

"Edward," I called softly. "Wait for me."

You annoying kid, I whispered to myself.

We walk through the town, past Potter's Jewels, Moxie's Market. We walk under a streetlight, and I look sideways at Edward. His mouth is set, like he's on a mission.

"Edward?"

"What?"

"It will be all right. Don't worry."

He looks quickly at me. Then he slows down.

"Okay," he says.

I can see his breath when he talks.

But after a moment, as if he can't help it, he is hurrying again.

We walk past The Cinema and Jack's bookstore with the dark windows. There are no cars. There are no people. It is the quietest place I have ever been. It is so quiet I can hear Edward breathing. He begins to hum a song.

"What are you humming?"

"'O Canada,'" he says. "I'm going to sing it first thing to Sabine when she's born. And then maybe the French national anthem."

We pass the last town streetlight, and then it is dark. Too dark to see Edward. But somehow I know he is smiling.

"Edward, Jake?"

The police car drove up beside us. Neither one of us had even noticed the lights of the car.

"What are you boys doing out here?" asked Tom. "It's two o'clock. And freezing."

Edward kept walking, so Tom cruised along beside us.

"We're going to the hospital. Maeve's having the baby," I said.

"Sabine," said Edward patiently.

"Ah, so it's a girl!" said Tom.

"It will be," said Edward.

"Get in, both of you. Get in!"

Edward hesitated.

Tom got out of the police car and opened the back door.

"You'll see her sooner, believe me."

Edward and I climbed into the backseat and we sped off. It was warm in the car.

"Can you sound the siren?" asked Edward.

Tom shook his head. "Don't think so."

He looked at Edward in his rearview mirror.

"But I can use the lights!" he said.

And then, as if it were a grand sign, we went to the hospital surrounded by light.

Chapter 10

The hospital lights were dimmed, and patients were asleep. Nurses moved down the hallways on rubber-soled shoes. No one cared that we were there in the middle of the night. The nurses acted as if children arrived every night, very late, to eat chips and drink cold soda out of machines and nap on tan couches.

No one said:

"You're too young to be here."

"Visiting hours are over."

"Who are you?"

"Go away."

"That is not allowed."

The nurse on duty told us that Maeve was

in the delivery room. The nurse's name tag said Angela Garden. She had long red curly hair, caught back in a barrette. Wisps of her hair fell down, touching her neck and her cheek.

"Does your father know you're here?" Angela asked with a smile. "And that you arrived very dramatically in a police car? I saw out the window."

We grinned at her, and she found us blankets and made us lie down.

"It could be hours," she said.

"It won't," said Edward. "It will be soon."

"Oh?"

Angela looked at me.

I shook my head.

"Don't ask me how he knows. He just knows," I said.

Angela looked at Edward.

"Some people just know things," she said thoughtfully.

Suddenly, she leaned over and kissed Edward, then me.

Edward smiled. I smiled, too.

Then Jack plunged out through the swinging doors and hugged us both.

"It's the middle of the night. How did you get here?" he asked.

"In a pumpkin coach," said Angela, "drawn by six white horses."

"I believe it," said Jack.

"We were walking. Tom picked us up," I said.

"Siren?" asked Jack.

"Lights!" said Edward happily.

"You know, I'm glad you're here," said Jack. "I usually don't have much company when a baby is born."

"There's always me," said Angela.

"Oh yes, there's always Angela," said Jack with a smile.

A nurse opened the door.

"Jack?"

"Oops, have to go. Later!" said Jack.

"Soon," said Edward. "You'll see us soon."

And as it turned out he was, Edward was, right again.

Edward was sleeping. I must have been sleeping, too, because all of a sudden there was a shadow over me. I opened my eyes. Angela. Jack stood beside her, the smallest thing in his arms, wrapped in a blanket.

"Edward."

I whispered his name. But Edward sat up as if I had yelled to him.

Jack sat down on the couch.

"I think you know already who this is," he said.

The baby was dressed in white, a small white knitted hat on her head. *Her?*

"Sabine," said Edward.

"Sabine," said Jack.

Edward smiled.

"We'll buy her red poppies," he said. "Sabine will love red poppies."

"I think it's Edward who loves red poppies," said Angela Garden.

And when Jack handed Sabine to Edward my throat felt tight. I remembered that day when I was three years old and Maeve had put Edward into my arms. Edward touched Sabine's face. And I didn't realize until Angela Garden put her arms around me that I was crying.

Night is almost over when Jack drives us home from the hospital. After we have said good-bye to Maeve and Angela Garden. After Edward has hummed "O Canada" to Sabine many times. Once, during that time, she opens her eyes and looks at Edward. Her eyes remind me of Edward's, not so blue as his, but as sharp and steady.

Jack turns into our driveway and parks the car. Early light touches the water.

And because Edward has asked for it, Jack walks down to the water. There is a whoosh of noise and a rocket shoots up above us all. A shower of sparks fills the sky. Fireworks. Sola, Wren and Will come running out of the house.

"Sabine is here!" calls Edward. "And she is more beautiful than any of us!"

Chapter 11

Sabine was noisy and funny. She liked music. Emmylou Harris excited her, and James Taylor. She waved her arms in a wild way when Carly Simon sang. She calmed, though, when Edward hummed "O Canada" to her. He hummed it softly and slowly, like a hymn. Sabine's eyes widened when she saw Edward.

"When will she smile?" asked Edward.

"She's too young," said Maeve. "But she'll do it one day. Don't worry."

"Do you think I could take a year off from school?" asked Edward very seriously. "So I could spend more time with her?"

Maeve was just as serious.

"No, Edward. That's not your job. Your job is to get educated. My job is to take care of Sabine."

"I like your job better," said Edward.

But it turned out that we all got more time with Sabine.

There was a huge water leak at our school. It would take a month or more to repair the fallen ceilings, the walls, the buckled floors. And to repair the pipes.

"A month more with Sabine," said Edward happily. "We will have baseball games when we can," he told her. "It's warm enough during the day. Baseball," he intoned loudly.

"She may be a baby, Edward. But she can hear you," said Sola grumpily.

"At least *you* can go to school," Maeve said to Sola.

Sola shrugged her shoulders.

"We'll do something fun every single day," said Jack. "I promise."

"Jack, Sabine needs a diaper change, I think," said Maeve. "Would you?"

"I'll do it!" cried Edward. "She likes it when I change her. We count her toes in French. Un, deux, trois . . ."

Wren rolled her eyes and Will counted with Edward.

". . . quatre, cinq, six, sept."

Edward grinned and plucked a diaper from a pile on the counter.

As he left, we all called after him:

"Huit, neuf, dix, onze . . . !"

We had baseball games because it was very warm for the fall. Sabine would sit on Albert Groom's lap as Edward called out his pitches to her from the pitcher's mound.

"Knuckleball!"

"Slider."

"Change up."

"That's a very bad habit, Edward," said Albert,

Sabine on his lap, looking at all that was in front of her: baseball, seawater, Weezer, and her favorite Edward.

"I won't do that when I pitch in the big leagues," called Edward, making Albert and Trick laugh.

"No, you won't," said Trick, making Albert laugh more.

For a while we could still have picnics and cookouts on the front lawn after baseball games, Sabine in her baby seat, waving her arms at us.

Edward sang a French song to her when he tired of "O Canada."

Sur le pont d'Avignon
L'on y danse, l'on y danse . . .

But Sabine was never tired of "O Canada." Finally Jack taught us the words and Edward made us all sing it before every baseball game.

And then it got too cold for baseball, though Edward would have played through northeasters and snow.

Edward and I took Sabine for walks in her stroller, with her snowsuit and knitted hat, down the sidewalks of the town, stopping every so often as people called "Sabine! Sabine!" from doorways and from across the street, running over to see her.

"Remember that night?" I asked Edward.

Edward knew what night I meant. It had been a month and a half ago.

"Yes," said Edward. "That's the night we met, Sabine. Do you remember that night?"

His voice rose and Sabine turned her head to find his face.

"And Angela Garden," I said, and Edward and I both laughed and couldn't stop.

Edward tried to teach Sabine how to throw a ball, but she was too young to care. Thanksgiving had gone, then Christmas. And Sabine smiled at

Edward all the time. Edward wrote that on his wall calendar. He also began to mark off the days until spring.

"Spring," he whispered to Sabine. "Baseball begins."

Chapter 12

Edward marked off the calendar days one by one. And then it was spring. Edward tried to teach Sabine how to crawl. Sabine got up on her hands and knees now and rocked.

"She'll crawl soon enough," said Maeve. "And there will be trouble."

"For now she's stuck in neutral," said Jack.

It rained in the morning of the first day of spring baseball, and then the sun came out. On the front porch Edward was having a discussion with Sabine about rainbows.

"Colors, we're looking for," he said. "Colors!"

He held her up, but all Sabine looked at was Edward. I could see the clouds and blue sky in her eyes—little globes of the world around her.

"Look, Sabine," said Edward. "There! Above the water. See? Blue, red, green? A sign!"

Sabine's drool fell on Edward's cheek, sitting there like a teardrop.

I laughed and leaned over to wipe it away.

"You and your signs, Edward."

Edward looked at me, Sabine's cheek next to his.

"You'll see one day, Jake. You'll see," said Edward.

Maeve banged pots in the kitchen as Nanci Griffith sang "Gulf Coast Highway" above the noise: "And when we die we say we'll catch some blackbird's wing."

Trick and Albert arrived early for lunch before the first afternoon baseball game.

"Opening day," said Albert happily.

Trick took Sabine's tiny hand in his big one.

"She's a lot bigger. And she looks like you, Edward," said Trick.

"Do you think?" said Edward.

Trick nodded.

"I think," he said.

Trick took some papers out of his jacket pocket.

"Here. Some pitching information. From the computer."

"Trick can find out anything. Anything in the world," said Albert. "Something for you to remember."

"You just have to ask the right questions," said Trick. He looked at me and winked. "Remember that, too. It's kind of magical, you know. You type in a question. It answers you. But you have to ask the right question."

Trick sat on a chair on the porch and took Sabine on his lap.

"The right question," he whispered to Sabine.

Her head bobbed as she stared at a button on Trick's shirt.

※ ※ ※

Things happen fast sometimes, Jack says that. Albert says it, too. On this day everything changes. It changes too fast; before anyone can say the things we should say.

Or see the things we should be looking at.

Or understand anything.

Or ask the right question.

Maeve brought out food for all of us on the porch, a big salad in a wooden bowl.

"Look at you, Sabine, with Uncle Trick!"

Jack brought a platter of sliced ham, with spiced apples scattered around the edges.

Edward ran down the yard and turned for a moment.

"I'll be back. I have to get something in town."

"What?" I asked.

"Come with me, Jake!" he called to me. "You'll see. We'll be right back."

"No, Edward. I don't want to. It's almost lunchtime."

Edward looked at me.

I shook my head.

"Why are you going?" I said.

"A surprise," called Edward happily. And he turned and ran down to our bikes, lying on the grass.

"Don't take your bike, Edward!" I called to him. "We never fixed those brakes."

Edward got on his bike and waved both of his hands in the air as he rode away.

"Edward!" I called.

His hands went up in the air again. I couldn't tell if he'd heard me. And then he was out of sight.

Out of sight. I think about riding after him for a moment. But Maeve calls to me and I don't follow him.

I don't follow him.

Chapter 13

"Where's that boy?" asked Maeve. She was dishing salad onto plates. "He's been gone for a long time."

Sabine sat on Albert Groom's lap. He bounced his knees lightly, chanting to her.

"This is the way the ladies ride,
   Trip, trip, trip.
   This is the way the gentlemen
     ride,
   TROT, TROT, TROT.
   This is the way the farmers
     ride,
   Hobbledy, hobbledy, hoy."

Sabine's mouth opened with happiness.

"Edward said he'd be back soon," said Wren. "Right, Jake?"

I nodded.

"He'll be back soon," said Will. "He loves ham."

"And baseball," said Albert Groom, smiling.

"And Sabine," I said.

Mary Brigid and Caitlin walked up the hill to our yard, Caitlin tossing her glove up and catching it. Weezer left his napping place under the porch, wagging his tail at them.

"He'd be back if I'd gone with him," I said, my voice fading as I watched a police car slowly drive into the yard. It stopped at the bottom of the yard.

"Is that Tom?" asked Jack, putting down his plate.

Jack began to walk down the yard. And then it was Tom who got out of the car. He stood by the hood, not moving. He had a small bag in his hand. Maeve went down the steps and caught up with Jack.

"Tom?" she said.

Her voice sounded very far away, as if she knew something she didn't want to know.

I stood at the edge of the steps. Sola moved next to me, so close our bodies touched. I could feel her begin to shake.

When Tom reached Maeve and Jack he took Maeve's hand and leaned down to speak to her. And then Maeve's knees buckled; she would have fallen if Jack hadn't gathered her up in his arms. Tom looked up at us up on the porch and started walking up the hill. Jack's arms were around Maeve and they stood there, not moving.

I started to walk down the stairs, but Albert Groom stopped me. He handed Sabine to me and he walked down to meet Tom. Sabine's head nestled in my neck. She was warm and smelled of something sweet. All of these things seemed so clear.

Tom touched Albert's arm gently as he

talked, Albert's head down as he listened. Then Tom handed Albert the paper bag. Behind him Maeve and Jack got into Tom's car, and they left. I thought, suddenly, maybe to keep other thoughts away, of the night that Edward and I watched a car leave and we walked to the hospital to see Sabine.

Albert stopped at the bottom of the steps. His face looked old and more lined than it had looked before.

"Edward's gone," he said.

He looked up at us then. Tears came down his face.

"I'm sorry," he whispered. "He's gone."

He handed me the paper bag and I opened it. It was a small blue baseball cap.

I couldn't speak. Gone where? I wanted to ask. But I knew. Before I began to cry I showed it to Sabine.

"This is for you," I said, my voice cracking into pieces. "From Edward."

*** * ***

We didn't eat. We couldn't talk. No one knew what to say. We moved past each other, putting food away. Trick and Albert swept the floor and cleaned off the table. And later Weezer, as if he knew something was wrong, came up to sit on the porch, leaning against Albert.

When Sabine began to fuss, Sola handed her to me.

"Sing to her," she said to me.

"But that's . . . ," I began.

A terrible silence filled the room.

Everyone knew what I was about to say. I was about to say that was Edward's job.

"I can't," I said. "I can't sing to her. It's my fault. It's all my fault!"

Sola put her arms around me.

The phone rang.

Albert answered.

"Yes? We're fine. All right."

He handed the phone to me.

"She wants to talk to you," he said.

"Hello?"

"Jake. It's Angela. Angela Garden. You remember?"

"Yes."

My voice didn't sound like mine.

"Your mother and father are on their way home. They had to make some decisions. But they're coming home."

I thought of Angela's red hair and how it lay against her cheek. Why was I thinking that?

"All right," I said.

"Jake?"

"Yes."

"I'm sorry. About what happened."

"Yes."

"Edward was a wonderful boy."

Was.

I hung up the phone without saying anything. Without saying good-bye or thank you.

All I could think of was that little word. So small.

Was.

So small.

And so big.

Chapter 14

Trick and Albert drank coffee in the kitchen. They were silent. Everything in the house was still. Wren was in her room, the door closed. Will, too. Sola had been gone for a long time. I walked out on the porch and saw her sitting down by the water, Sabine on her lap. I walked down the steps and down the grass, wet with early dew now. I stepped over second base and my throat tightened up. I could feel tears at the corners of my eyes.

I stood next to Sola for a moment. The sky was flat dark blue, no clouds. She didn't look up at me. I sat down next to her. She turned then, and her face didn't seem like Sola's face anymore.

It looked like stone. It frightened me. Sabine made small baby sounds between us. A herring gull wheeled over the water and I thought about the day Edward had hit a long ball where the gull had flown. A sign.

We sat for a long time, not speaking. And then we heard a car. We stood and watched Tom's police cruiser come into the driveway. Jack got out of the backseat and reached out his hand to help Maeve. Tom got out, too, and went up to Maeve and held her hand, just the way he had when he came to get them and take them away. Then Tom got into his car and left. Maeve and Jack walked up the yard, holding hands. Jack turned and saw us then, and they stopped. No one said anything. *Wasn't anyone going to say something? Anything?*

Maeve's eyes were red rimmed and that frightened me as much as Sola's stone face had frightened me.

"Oh, Sabine," she whispered.

She took Sabine. Then she put her arms around me and I began to cry so hard that she handed Sabine to Jack and held me tighter, as if she knew I might break into a thousand pieces if she didn't.

"Come. Into the house," she said softly.

Jack took Sola's hand. We walked up to the porch and into the house.

Albert and Trick stood up.

"Maeve . . . ," Albert began, his voice breaking. "We'll go now."

"No." Maeve's voice was stronger now.

"Thank you for staying," said Jack. "Thank you so much." He put Sabine into her high chair.

Wren and Will had heard Tom's car. They stood in the kitchen doorway. Maeve hugged them both.

"I want you to stay, Albert. Trick. I want to tell you what happened."

Albert filled a glass of water and handed it to Maeve.

"Thank you, Albert."

She looked up at Albert standing next to her.

"What would we do without you?" she said, her eyes filling up with tears.

Jack put his head down on his arms for a moment. And there was silence again. Late afternoon light fell across the kitchen table. Maeve got up and turned on a lamp.

I waited for her to speak. But I couldn't wait any longer.

"It was the brakes of the bike, wasn't it? I told him not to go. I should have followed him. . . ."

Maeve held up her hand with a fierce look. Sabine's hand went up to Albert's cheek.

"Could? Should?" said Maeve, her voice flat. "I could have told Edward not to go to town, Jake. Maybe I should have."

She took a sip of her water.

"I bet you already thought about that. Didn't you?"

My face got hot.

I had thought of that.

"It's all right, Jake. You haven't thought anything that hasn't gone through my mind today, either."

She stroked my hair.

"Now. We won't talk about 'woulds' or 'coulds,'" she went on.

"We will talk about Edward," she said softly.

Chapter 15

Wren came over and leaned on Trick. He put an arm around her. Will sat across from me. Sola stood at the sink, so still.

Maeve began.

"Edward died at one o'clock this afternoon," she said flatly.

I could hear Sola take in a breath. It was the first time it had been said. Edward's gone, Albert had said. Gone meant he was somewhere to be found. Dead meant dead.

"One o'clock," I whispered.

"Game time," said Jack, taking my hand. "If you're thinking that, it's all right."

"It wasn't anyone's fault that he died," said Maeve. "There's no one to blame."

"It wasn't the brakes of his bike, Jake," said Jack. "No one ran into him. He turned on his bike to wave and smile at someone across the street."

"I can see him doing that," Maeve whispered. "And he ran into a tree. And that was all. No one knows why he went to town."

"He went to get a baseball cap. That one," I said. "For Sabine."

Maeve picked up the cap and and put it up to her cheek.

"And we can't blame Sabine, either," she said. "Can we."

Wren began to cry. Trick gathered her onto his lap and held her.

"So, he's just gone. Like that?" said Will angrily. "Gone forever?"

Maeve took a deep breath.

"Yes," she said. "And no."

✳ ✳ ✳

They have taken Edward's heart. And his lungs and other organs to give people who need them. Even his tissue they've taken. Maeve tells us this is like Edward living on. No, I want to say. It is not like Edward living on. Where is he? I want to yell at her. They've taken all of him. Where is Edward!?

"And there's one thing more," said Maeve, looking at me.

"We have donated Edward's corneas."

I jumped up from the table, my chair crashing on the floor behind me. Sabine began to cry.

"Why did you do that?" I yelled at Maeve. "I hate you for doing that!"

Albert Groom put his arms around me and held me close. I fought him at first. Then I gave up and cried.

"No!" I said into his shirt. "They are Edward's eyes!"

Albert turned and walked me to the kitchen

door and out onto the porch, closing the door behind us.

After a minute he leaned down close to my ear. I could feel the tears on his face. He whispered so softly that I leaned back and looked at him to hear better.

"Someone should have those wonderful eyes," he said softly. "Someone who needs them."

I stared at him.

Then he looked over my head out to the water.

"Remember what Trick once said? You have to ask the right questions."

"I would ask why did Edward die," I said.

Albert sighed.

"Maybe. But maybe the right question now is what would Edward want?"

I went over to the porch railing and looked out to the baseball field. No players. Only Weezer sitting down by the water waiting for something.

"Weezer looks like he's waiting for something," I said. "A sign."

Behind me Albert Groom's voice was clear and steady.

"I think we're all waiting for a sign," he said sadly.

Chapter 16

It was quiet for days. There was no laughter in our house and no talk. Silence filled all the spaces, taking up all the air.

Flowers were delivered. Food arrived.

But no music.

"Maeve doesn't sing," I said to Jack.

"She will, Jake. When the right time comes."

"What's the right time?" I asked him.

"It will come," was all he said.

He put his arms around me.

"I promise," he said very softly.

Will packed up all his books in boxes and put them under his bed.

"I don't want to read," he told me.

Wren was quiet.

"Want to go to town, Wren? We'll have ice cream," I said.

Wren shook her head.

"It's too scary," she said.

I had no answer for her.

Some nights Maeve took walks. I saw her from my window. And once when I passed Edward's room she was there, sitting on his bed, slowly turning the pages of *Goodnight Moon*. She never saw me standing in the doorway. I wanted her to look up, smile at me, and beckon me in to sit by her. But she didn't. So I made her hear me.

"I taught him how to read," I said, my voice loud in the quiet room.

Maeve jumped a bit, startled.

"And I sat with him in the bathroom, and read him that book." I pointed.

"Even in French, and I taught him baseball rules, and . . ." I couldn't go on.

Maeve got up and put her arms around me.

"Oh, Jake, it was as if he was yours from the very beginning," she said. "You raised him."

I looked at her, surprised.

"He loved you," said Maeve. "Maybe he never said it. But it was you he came to for everything."

She looked down at me.

"I'm so sad for you, Jake," she said.

I started to cry again.

"You know what?" I said after a while.

"What?"

"I'm mad at Edward," I said. "For running into that tree."

Maeve sighed.

"I am, too," she said. "I am, too," she repeated very softly.

"Edward was special," I said.

Maeve looked closely at me.

"Of course he was. Like you and Sola and Wren and Will and Sabine . . ."

"No," I said. "He was different. He was more special."

Maeve looked surprised.

"Here's what I think, Jake. If Edward seemed more special, maybe it was because of you."

Suddenly, I thought about Edward, curled up next to me, falling asleep on the lawn. I could almost . . . *almost* smell him.

Maeve and I sat on Edward's bed then for a long, long time. In that quiet empty room.

Sola carried Sabine into my room.

"I miss everything. I even miss the baseball games," she said.

"You miss Edward," I whispered. It was hard to say. My throat ached.

"Yes. And I miss the way things were," she said.

I reached out my hand and touched Sabine's cheek. She moved her head and looked at me. Her eyes were steady and serious. Sabine's eyes and Edward's eyes were all mixed up in my mind.

Edward's eyes.

✳ ✳ ✳

That night I dreamed about them, looking at me, that gold-flecked blue of the night sky when he was a baby. Looking at me across the yard—across the water after he dove from the boat—from the pitcher's mound as he called out his strikes, "change up, slider, knuckleball." I woke up from my dream and had to get out of bed and walk through the house to keep my heart from beating too fast.

It was a sign, that dream. Trick would have said so. Edward would have said so, too.

Two days later the letter came.

Chapter 17

It was late afternoon, Trick and Albert cooking a stew in the kitchen, my mother trying to save some of the flowers that had come, tossing out the ones that had gone by. Jack came in, carrying a small glass vase and holding a letter.

"I found these flowers on the porch," he said. "Someone must have left them."

"Poppies," said Maeve, with a small smile. The first smile I had seen in days. "Beautiful red poppies, almost ready to bloom."

Red poppies.

"Who left them?" asked Sola. "We've been here all day."

Maeve shook her head. "I didn't see anyone."

Jack put the vase in the middle of the table.

He took Maeve's hand.

"They gave me this letter. At the hospital," he said. "It's for us. You'll want to read it."

We all looked up at the strange, sad sound of his voice.

Maeve read it in the kitchen, the letter trembling in her hands. Trick and Albert stopped cooking, leaning against the counter, listening. Wren and Will sat at the table. Wren reached out for Sabine. Sabine touched Wren's hair.

"Dear friends,

They won't tell me your name, as you know. But I call you friends even though I don't know you.

The corneas you have donated have brought back my life. I am a baseball player . . . minor league right now . . . but my eyes were getting worse.

You have changed my life. And I thank you from the bottom of my heart. I hope some day I can thank you in person.

I know you must have loved the person who gave me these wonderful eyes."

Maeve sat down suddenly as if she couldn't stand anymore. She dropped the letter on the table.

"It's a nice letter," said Jack softly.

"Yes," said Maeve. "Yes," she whispered. "I don't know how to feel . . . sad or glad."

"Both," said Trick. "Both," he repeated softly.

A baseball player. Of all the people in the world; painters, writers, mechanics, builders, teachers, waiters, dancers, singers, librarians, mothers, fathers, sisters, brothers . . .

A baseball player!

❊ ❊ ❊

Albert reached over to look at the letter.

"He doesn't play too far away," he said with a small smile.

He handed the letter to Trick.

"Close enough," said Trick.

I looked at the name at the bottom of the letter: Willie Roberts.

It was quiet. And in that quiet something happened. A poppy bud in the vase trembled a little. As we watched, the husk fell to the table and very, very slowly the poppy opened.

Sabine turned to look. And then another trembled. The husk fell, and the flower slowly, more slowly than the first flower, opened. None of us moved or spoke. And then Sabine made a small chirp.

A sign. You know it when you see it.

I stood up.

"Music," I said to Maeve. "It's a sign. Please. Please, we need music," I pleaded. "*Sabine* needs music."

Maeve looked up at me for a moment. Then she got up and put a disc into the player.

Suddenly, music filled the room. Sabine waved her arms.

"Good night, you moonlight ladies. Rockabye sweet baby James."

Jack put his arms around Maeve and they danced.

Wren got up and danced with Sabine. Maeve reached out and took Sabine, dancing with her and Jack. Maeve smiled and cried at the same time. And she began to sing, softly at first. Sabine smiled her toothless smile, and then, with her eyes on Maeve, Sabine laughed.

That sound, so new, made us all laugh. *Something about that sound.* I looked at Will and I could see the change in his look. Wren was different. Her worried look was gone.

Maeve put in another disc.

I went out to the porch, the sound of music following me.

"And when we die we say we'll catch some blackbird's wing."

Albert came out, too.

I leaned down and picked up a small card that had dropped there.

It read:

The poppies are in memory of
Edward. He loved them.
—Angela Garden

I smiled.

The door opened behind me, and everyone came out and down the yard to the water.

And then, for Edward, because he had once said he wanted it, Jack sent off a rocket. It went high in the sky over the water, a big dandelion of light. Albert and I watched the sparks fall back to the water. Then it was quiet again.

"I want to find them," I said.

"Them?"

I looked at Albert.

"Edward's eyes," I said.

"We will," said Albert, putting his arm around me. "We surely will."

Epilogue

Willie was three for four. One was a pop-up and I thought about when I taught Edward the infield fly rule, reading to him in the bathroom. I remembered Edward calling it to me from the baseball field in our front yard.

His last time at bat Willie hit to the opposite field. A solid drive.

"Good eyes," said Albert under his breath.

Then he looked at me, suddenly knowing what he had said.

"It's okay," I said softly.

When the game was over and we got up to leave, Willie came up to us.

"This is Trick and Albert," I said. "They played baseball."

"I could tell," said Willie. "By your throw," he said to Albert.

Albert smiled.

"You had a good day," said Albert.

Willie nodded.

"Better every day now," he said, still looking at me.

I stared at his eyes, looking for Edward there. But somehow, the eyes that looked back at me were Willie's eyes.

When we started to go, Willie called to us.

"Will you come again?" he asked.

"Yes," I answered before Trick and Albert could answer.

Willie came over and put his arms around me.

"Thank you," he said softly.

Albert Groom drove home, Trick in the front seat, me in the back. I watched trees and houses go by, a pond and a marsh, tall cattails at the edges.

"Albert?"

Albert looked in the rearview mirror at me.

"Yes?"

"I think we should start the baseball games again."

"Good idea," said Albert.

There was a silence.

"And . . . ," I paused.

"Yes, Jake."

"Maybe I'll play baseball," I said, surprising myself.

Trick turned to smile at me.

"Okay," said Albert.

There was another long silence. I saw the bay off in the distance. Soon we'd be home. We rounded the head of the bay, light sitting on water.

"Maybe I'll learn how to throw a knuckleball," I said very softly from the backseat.

No one said anything. Maybe no one heard me.

We drove into the driveway and got out of the car.

Albert held up his hand for a high five. He'd heard me.

We were home.